The
WITCHES
of
BENEVENTO

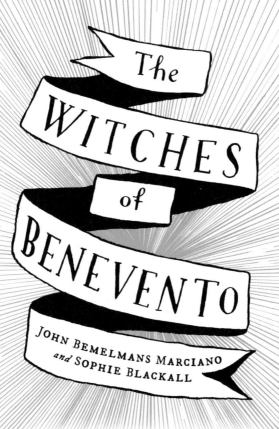

The WITCHES of BENEVENTO

JOHN BEMELMANS MARCIANO and SOPHIE BLACKALL

MISCHIEF SEASON

A Twins Story

VIKING

VIKING

An imprint of Penguin Random House LLC
375 Hudson Street
New York, New York 10014

First published in the United States of America by Viking,
an imprint of Penguin Random House LLC, 2016

LIBRARY OF CONGRESS CATALOGING-IN-PUBLICATION DATA IS AVAILABLE.
ISBN: 978-0-451-47181-9

1 3 5 7 9 10 8 6 4 2

Manufactured in China   Set in IM FELL French Canon
Book design by Nancy Brennan

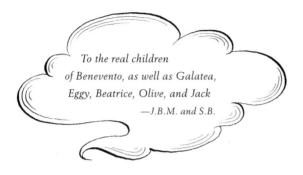

To the real children
of Benevento, as well as Galatea,
Eggy, Beatrice, Olive, and Jack
— J.B.M. and S.B.

Emilio

Rosa

Primo

Maria Beppina

Sergio

CONTENTS

OPENING NOTE 1

MAP OF BENEVENTO 4

1 ⚜ *Stealing Cheese* 11

2 ⚜ *Counting Salt* 19

3 ⚜ *Crying Janara* 29

4 ⚜ *Zia Pia* 35

5 ⚜ *Bloo Bloe Blee Blie!* 45

6 ⚜ *Ish Ka-Bibble* 51

7 ⚜ *The Tree of the Janara* 65

8 ⚜ *Amerigo Pegleg* 85

9 ⚜ *A Whiff of Oregano* 101

CLOSING NOTE 112

WITCHONARY 114

HOW THEY LIVED 116

HISTORICAL NOTE 118

Dear Reader,

Benevento is an ordinary place, except for one extraordinary thing: it has more witches than anywhere else in the whole entire world.

Does the word "witch" make you think of cackling, green-skinned, broom-riding hags? Well, the Witches of Benevento are nothing like that.

Here in Benevento, a witch can be any sort of supernatural creature. There are spirits, fairies, ghosts, and demons—such as yours truly—as well as those you may never have heard of, like the Manalonga and the Clopper. And then there are the Janara.

A Janara may be anyone you know—your next-door neighbor, your uncle, or even your mom. After the rest of the world has gone to sleep, Janara rub a secret oil on their armpits and say a spell, thus transforming themselves. They gain the power not only to fly but to control the weather itself!

Despite their amazing powers, Janara steer clear of people (at least those who are awake) lest they be grabbed by the hair and can't return to their bodies by dawn, in which case they must stay in their witch form forever.

Janara come out whenever it is stormy, or whenever it is Mischief Season. Mischief Season comes four times a year, but is most unpredictable during spring. In spring, even the nicest Janara might be tempted to sneak into the rooms of sleeping children to play mischiefs. (And you don't even _want_ to know what the mean ones do!)

Against such mischiefs, you must

take precautions. Unfortunately, natural disasters can't completely be prevented, be they tornado, flood, or Janara.

So, children, prepare yourselves! And hope that you may <u>never</u> be the unlucky target of a mischiefing Janara, unlike the twins you are about to meet. They are able children, to be sure, but what chance have they against the power of the Witches?

Your loyal servant,
Sigismondo
(with Bruno & Rafaella)

THE WITCHES
of
BENEVENTO

When you hear the Clopper's **clop clop clop***,*

Run through the Theater and never stop.

Keep far from Bridges and from Wells,

Where Manalonga love to dwell.

If you are good and do your chores,

The Janara won't get you while you snore.

Respect your Ghosts and love your Sprites,

Kiss your Mom and say Good Night.

MISCHIEF SEASON

A Twins Story

1
STEALING CHEESE

"UGH!"

That's the word Rosa wakes up saying.

Her stomach—it's all twisted into knots! The pain is part like a stomachache and part like she's starving. But Rosa never gets sick, and how the heck could she be hungry? She had a full dinner *and* snuck downstairs before bed to eat a whole ball of cheese.

Then there's her nose! It feels so uncontrollably, unbearably, can't-*stop*-it-ly itchy. Not just at the tip, either, but all the way up inside and back down her throat.

The strangest thing, though, is that she woke up before her brother. That *never* happens.

"Emilio!" She shakes her twin, lying next to her. Geez, does he snore loudly! "Come on, wake up!"

Rosa tells Emilio about her stomachache.

"Well, maybe that'll teach you not to eat a pound of cheese right before you go to sleep." He rubs his eyes. "You're going to get in trouble for that, you know."

"No, I won't." Rosa smirks. "A Janara did it!"

A Janara did it! is Rosa's excuse for everything. As far as excuses go, it's a really, really good one. Stealing cheese is, in fact, exactly the kind of thing a Janara does.

Janara sneak into houses during the night and do all kinds of mischiefs, usually to kids and sometimes to animals. It's still too early in the spring for Mischief Season, but that isn't going to stop Rosa from blaming the Janara.

The person you have to guard your food against at the Twins' house isn't a witch, however. It's Rosa herself. When Rosa is hungry—which is most of the time—she'll steal the food right off your plate. Like this morning.

Momma is braiding Rosa's hair when she reaches across the table to grab a crust from her little brother's dish.

"Hey!" Dino says. "That was mine!"

"So... 'ungry..." Rosa says as she stuffs her mouth.

"Whoa, daughter!" Momma says, pulling back on Rosa's braids like the reins of a horse. "Calm down and let me get you some cheese, dear."

With her big round ball of a pregnant belly leading the way, Momma goes over to where the cheeses are hanging from the rafters. She can't find the one she's looking for.

HEY!

Rosa stops chewing, takes a big gulp, and looks down guiltily.

"Rosa!" her mother says. "Did you eat an *entire* cheese last night?"

"No way, Momma!" she says. "A Janara must have done it!"

BANG!

Father's fist hits the table. The silverware and plates all jump and jangle.

He then draws down the corner of his right eyelid with his index finger—his warning to watch out.

"No. More. Janara."

Father barely ever talks, and when he does, it is one word at a time. But he always gets his point across. He doesn't want to hear Rosa's excuses anymore.

Rosa gulps again. But this time she doesn't have any food in her mouth.

2

COUNTING SALT

ROSA'S itchy nose and stomachache aren't the only odd things going on around the farm. By this point in the spring, there should be lots of wild greens to take to market, but all Rosa and Emilio can find in the fields is some scraggly crow's garlic. The fog isn't helping either.

"Where are the eggs?" Rosa asks Dino as Emilio loads the oxcart.

"The hens aren't laying!" he says. "Don't blame me—it must still be too cold out."

If not for Emilio's side business in mushrooms (he hunts them in the woods on his own time), it wouldn't even be worth making the morning delivery to Cousin Primo's stand.

"What's wrong with you?" Primo says to Rosa when they arrive. "You look awful. Even worse than usual."

Primo smirks that smug Primo smirk of his, the one when he thinks he's being *so* clever. Which he never is.

Rosa, who usually gives at least as good as she gets, just sticks out her tongue at her cousin and taps Ugo the ox with the whip to get moving.

Passing through the city gate, Emilio makes the horns with his fingers and spits, warding off the nasty spirit who resides there. A freezy spring drizzle starts up, spurring

LA·LA·LA·LA·LA

Ugo to break into a trot. His hooves go ***bang-bang-bang***ing against the stones of the bridge while Emilio sticks his fingers in his ears and sings *LA-la-la-la-La!* He elbows his sister to do the same—does she want the Manalonga to get her?—but Rosa just gives him a dirty look and holds her stomach. Emilio sighs. His twin is going to get herself in real trouble one of these days.

"Can you at least stop picking your nose?" he says.

"I'm not picking!" she says. "I'm *rubbing*. It's still itchy."

The next morning, Emilio gets woken up by another furious shake. "Emilio! Emilio! It happened again!"

The sheets are all damp. *"Skeevo!"* Emilio says. "Did you wet the bed?"

"No, donkey-brains! It was the mares!" Rosa says, soaked with sweat and shaking. It looks like she just took a bath. (Which would be weird enough. Rosa hates baths.) "I was attacked by mares!"

Mares are the worst! They are goblins who sneak into the house alongside Janara and sit on your chest so you can't breathe. The thing is, mares can only get into your house if Janara *let* them in.

"It was just a bad dream," Emilio says.

"No! I have the same stomachache again, too. And my nose is on fire!" She grabs it. "It feels like it was scraped out with a shovel."

Now Emilio is intrigued. "Maybe it really *is* the Janara. They might be using a straw."

"What?" Rosa says, alarmed.

"When Janara are really hungry—or really nasty—they sit on your chest, stick a straw up your nose, and suck all the food out of your belly. Primo's grandma told me about it, and she knows *everything* about witches."

"That's exactly what it feels like!" Rosa says. "But it's too early for Janara, isn't it?"

"Maybe Mischief Season came early this year." Emilio shrugs.

"Well, why aren't they doing anything to *you*?"

"That's a good question," Emilio says, and starts to get dressed, thinking. Emilio likes thinking. Especially about mysteries.

"Salt," he says. "We need salt."

BONG BONG BONG

"What did you say?!"

Primo can't hear Emilio because of the ringing of the mid-morning bell—his family's grocery stand is right next to the cathedral—so Emilio again explains the goings-on of the previous night.

"Fan-*tas*-tic!" Primo says. "Janara!"

"It is *not* fantastic," Rosa says, hunched over with stomach cramps.

Game for any scheme, Primo scoops a small sack of salt out of the barrel for the Twins. He scrapes the sides to mound the salt up in the middle so his father won't be able to tell. Not that he would even get into trouble—Primo's poppa is the complete opposite of the Twins'. He lets Primo do *anything.* Lucky!

Before bed, Emilio starts dividing the salt into little bags to put on windowsills and hang off the doorknob. You can't stop Janara from getting into your room at night—they are made of wind and just blow through the keyhole—but you *can* keep them busy.

Janara are obsessive counters, as anyone in Benevento can tell you. When Janara come across a bag of salt, they have to open it and count out every last tiny grain. And when they're done, they have to do it a *second* time, just to be sure. They never finish by the dawn bell, at which time they have to leave and go back to their regular bodies. If they don't, they'll never be able to return at all.

"Come on and help me," Emilio says to his sister.

Rosa groans and holds her stomach. "I *can't!*" she says, her ache suddenly worse. Or so she acts. It's always the same with her, Janara or no Janara—any excuse to get out of work.

Dino helps, at least. As a final touch, Emilio gets some cheese and a glass of wine. Janara are known to get hungry when they go mischiefing but they will sometimes skip houses that have a nice snack laid out.

Emilio wakes up the next morning to the rooster's crow, turns over, and sees his sister still asleep. A string of drool connects the corner of her mouth to the mattress .

"Rosa! Rosa!" He shakes her. "Wake up!"

"What? Why?" she says, shutting her eyes tighter.

"The Janara—did they come last night? Can you feel anything?"

Rosa sits up in bed, eyes wide open. "I feel great!" She touches her nose, then her belly. "In fact, I don't feel anything at all!"

"And look!" Emilio says, pointing at the empty plate and glass. "They ate the cheese and drank the wine!"

The Twins are both quite pleased with themselves.

Until:

"Rosaaaaaa!"

3
CRYING JANARA

IT is a bad thing when Father yells. It's a bad thing when *any* parent yells, but it's especially bad with this one.

"Rosa!" he yells again.

Rosa gets half dressed and goes outside to where Father is standing, with Emilio close behind. Father doesn't say another word, he just walks to the barn. The Twins follow.

Inside, every tool lies scattered on the ground. Even the pitchforks—tines up. All the animals' water buckets have been turned upside down and the hay taken out of the stalls and scattered in the aisle.

The Twins protected their room so well

that the Janara moved out to the barn.

Father stands there, staring at Rosa, fuming.

"But I didn't do anything! It was a Ja—"

Father holds up a finger in front of her mouth to stop her from saying another word. His face is red with anger.

"But—"

Father turns even redder, and gives her the warning sign with his eye.

The problem is that, even though Rosa hasn't done anything, it is all the sort of thing she has done *on occasion*, whether by mistake, or during a game, or because she was lazy.

Once Rosa took Father's entire toolbox into the woods without asking—she wanted to build a tree house—and left it there in the rain, where it all rusted over by morning. She blamed a Janara, and even though he figured she was fibbing, Father couldn't say for sure that a Janara *didn't* do it, so he never punished her. Now, however, Rosa has blamed Janara too many times for him to bear.

"That's it!" Emilio says as Father stalks away.

"What?" Rosa says.

"You've cried wolf."

"What?" she says again.

"Don't you see? Father is sick of you blaming the Janara, but the Janara are sick of you blaming them, too. That's why they are doing this to you—for revenge!"

"You mean, they *want* me to get into trouble?"

BONG BONG BONG

This time the mid-morning bell drowns out Primo's laugh.

"The Janara are messing with Rosa because of her *excuses*!" Primo tells Sergio and Maria Beppina when they arrive. "Isn't that the funniest thing you ever *heard*?"

Rosa is so mad she punches Primo in the arm.

"Don't get mad at me!" Primo says. "Get mad at the Janara."

"I *am* mad at the Janara," Rosa says, shaking her fist in the air. "If they had the guts to come out during the day, I'd show them some *real* mischiefs!"

"Can't you put a bag of salt in the barn like you did in your bedroom?" Maria Beppina asks.

"That only works inside," Emilio says. "It's a rule."

"Sometimes I think my mom is a Janara," Sergio says. "She is so mean."

"But Janara aren't usually mean," Emilio says. "You have to *do* something to make them mad."

"I wonder who your Janara is," Maria Beppina says. "In real life, I mean."

"We just have to figure out who really doesn't like Rosa," Sergio says.

"That could be *any*body!" Primo says, and Rosa slugs him in the arm again.

"Look, none of this is going to help," Emilio says. "We have to talk to someone who knows about Janara."

Everyone shudders, because they know exactly who Emilio means: **Zia Pia**.

4
ZIA PIA

THE home of Zia Pia lies in the walls of the Theater, and to get there, you have to outrun that crazy old witch, the Clopper. (They call her that because of her one wooden clog that goes *clop clop clop*.)

For Rosa, this is a snap. She's the fastest kid around, a fact that drives Primo nuts. To make him even *more* nuts, Rosa lets Primo get right up next to her, and even a *tiny* bit ahead. At the last minute, she turns on the speed and leaves him in her dust. She almost feels bad about it.

Almost.

Emilio and Sergio follow, with Maria Beppina coming in a distant last—always last. They all breathe hard from the run.

A little harder than usual, because of what is looming before them: the long staircase that leads to the parlor of Zia Pia, fortune-teller and spell-maker.

"Are we *sure* we should do this?" Sergio says.

None of the kids has ever been inside of Zia Pia's house, but they all have an aunt or uncle who has paid her to take off the evil eye, or talk to a dead relative, or find a piece of lost jewelry. The Twins' momma just went to her for a potion that would make her stop throwing up from being pregnant.

"Zia Pia will definitely know what

to do," Rosa says. "I hear she's a real Janara."

"She can't be a Janara," Emilio says. "Janara *never* tell anyone who they are."

"*She* didn't say she was. Other people do."

"*Go back! Go back!*" The kids hear a spooky voice. "*Go back* while you still can!"

GO BACK!

The kids turn to see Amerigo Pegleg, sitting outside his one-room apartment under the stairs, leaning on his cane and grinning at having scared them.

"Don't be afraid of that old pirate!" Primo says, and charges up the steps.

Emilio and Maria Beppina start slowly walking up, but not Sergio.

"Y'know, I think I hear Bis-Bis ringing his bell," Sergio says, referring to the ghost who lives upstairs from him. Sergio has to do whatever his ancestor spirit asks, but he also uses Bis-Bis as an all-purpose excuse. "I'd better go see what he wants."

"No, you don't, you big faker," Rosa says, and lifts Sergio by the collar to drag him up the steps.

Inside it is dark. *Really* dark. An olive-oil lamp gives off just enough light to make out the pinched, sour face of Zia Pia, who is seated at a table. On the table are an empty bowl, a bottle of water, and some tarot cards.

"What do you *children* want?" Zia Pia says, like the word *children* is the worst insult in the world.

"We . . ." Emilio says, "we want to talk about Janara."

"Talking isn't free."

"I have money," Emilio says, pulling a lumpy bag out of one of his pockets.

"I don't want your worthless copper quattrini," the old fortune-teller says.

"These coins are silver," Emilio says, holding out a shiny scudo for her to see.

At the sight of the silver coin, Zia Pia's eyes open wide and the flame of the lamp dances off them.

"*Silver*? How many mushrooms have you *picked*?" Sergio says, as surprised as Zia Pia to see Emilio with such a coin.

"I know why you have come. Mischiefs!" She smiles. "The Janara are mysterious and you shall never know their ways. Lucky for you that I do!"

Zia Pia takes her cards and turns over a queen.

"Have you ever heard of the witch Circe?" she says, pointing at the card. "She turned the crew of Ulysses into beasts—a most powerful mischief!"

Zia Pia now lays down a king.

"Ulysses beat her magic with an herb as common as it is powerful: wild garlic."

"We have lots of crow's garlic!" Rosa says. "That's the only thing growing."

"Heed my words and do exactly as I instruct, children," she says.

"You must get:

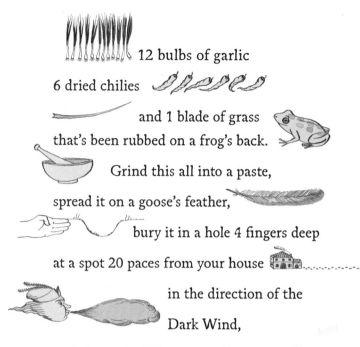

12 bulbs of garlic

6 dried chilies

and 1 blade of grass that's been rubbed on a frog's back. Grind this all into a paste, spread it on a goose's feather, bury it in a hole 4 fingers deep at a spot 20 paces from your house in the direction of the Dark Wind, and chant the following spell 3 times:

"Shoo, shoo, Janara, shoo!
Blee Blie Bloe Bloo!
Slime of frogs and pepper's fire,
Leave us for the muck and mire!"

The kids begin to shout out questions, but Zia Pia just snatches the silver coin from Emilio's hand and kicks them out of her house.

5

BLOO BLOE BLEE BLIE!

MOST of the ingredients are no problem to get. Wild garlic is sprouting in every field and Momma has bunches of dried chili peppers hanging from the rafters. As for the feather, the butcher is all too happy to let them pluck one off a dead goose. The last item, however, is not so easy.

"Dang frog!" Rosa says, as yet another one slips out of her hands. "We're never going to catch one!"

Rosa's whole body is splattered with stinky river mud, and she and Emilio are alone. The other kids all gave up a while ago and went home to dinner.

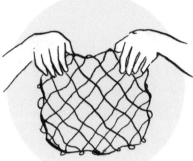

"Can you stop knitting like an old lady and *help* me?" Rosa says to her twin brother.

"Actually, I just finished," Emilio says, and holds up the net he's made to admire it. He then attaches the long strings from its corners to a stick and lays it out on a lily pad.

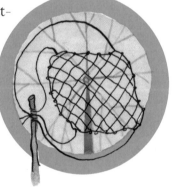

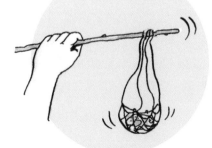

"Aw, that's never going to—"

"Work?" Emilio says, just as a frog

lands on the net and he yanks up the stick. The frog swings in the trap like a baby in a sack.

Back home, Emilio swabs the frog's back with a blade of grass and grinds it into the mixture with the other ingredients, which he slathers onto the goose feather. Rosa marches twenty paces from the house but Emilio has to redo it.

"Why?" Rosa says.

"Because the Dark Wind isn't *that* way," he says, pointing. "It's *that* way."

"Aw, what's the difference!"

Emilio digs a short trench in the ground until it measures four fingers deep, then puts the feather in. As he pats the dirt down he starts to speak the spell, but Rosa breaks in and says, "I wanna say it! You already got to do all the mixing and the digging."

"But that was only because you were too lazy," Emilio says. "Saying the spell is the fun part!"

Rosa hurries and says,

"Shoo, shoo, Janara, shoo!
Bloo Bloe Blee Blie!
Slime of frogs and Pepper's fire,
Leave us for the muck and mire!"

"That's not right!" Emilio says. "*Shoo* and *Blie* don't even rhyme! It's *Blee Blie Bloe **Bloo**!*"

"Was too right!" Rosa says.

Emilio says the spell the way Zia Pia said it, but can barely hear himself for Rosa shouting her version of the spell over him.

In bed, Rosa says, "Well, that's that! No more Janara problems." And she goes to sleep.

Emilio never gets to sleep that easily. Things never get fixed that easily, either.

6

ISH KA-BIBBLE

NEXT morning.

"Rosaaaaa!"

"Do you think it worked?" Rosa says to Emilio as they jump out of bed.

"What do *you* think?" he says.

They find Father in the barn. The animals are in their stalls, with water and hay still in their proper places. Poca the mule, however, is drenched in sweat, like she was ridden hard all night—exactly a Janara kind of mischief. Unfortunately, it is again also a Rosa kind of mischief.

This time Father is *really* mad. The kind of mad the Twins have never seen before. He's

convinced Rosa is to blame, even though Momma believes now it really *is* a Janara. Rosa gets a spanking. Worse, she gets grounded.

"**Forever!**" Father says.

Rosa isn't allowed to leave the farm, not even to take Ugo the ox into town. Instead, she has to pick rocks from the furrows Father plows while Emilio does the deliveries. And no going out after work to play. Or anything.

"It's not FAIR!" Rosa says, and sulks. Emilio feels bad for his sister, but what can he

do? He loads the cart—not that there is much to take—and heads off alone to Primo's stand.

"That rotten old fortune-teller!" Primo says after hearing what happened. "She can't give us some worthless spell and take our money!"

"*My* money, you mean," Emilio says.

This time, the long staircase up to Zia Pia's isn't empty. There are three people waiting. At the back of the line is Paulo Pasquarelli, a tall beanpole of a farmer who lives just downriver from the Twins.

"And then *this* morning, I found all the ox harnesses hanging in the treetops!" Farmer Paulo says. "I just can't take it anymore!"

"And we thought it was just *our* farm," Emilio says.

"Heck no!" the man at the front of the line says. "I woke up this morning and found my outhouse turned upside down. And it's made of stone!"

"Looks like it's going to be the worst Mischief Season ever," Farmer Paulo says.

"If all you farmers are so keen on giving your money away," Amerigo Pegleg hollers from his usual seat, "why don't you give it to *me* instead of that old fraud upstairs?" He chuckles.

When their turn finally comes, Emilio starts telling Zia Pia what happened.

"It didn't *work*!" Primo says, cutting him off. "We want our money back!"

"You foolish boys! Of course the spell worked," Zia Pia says. "Do you have any idea how much *worse* the mischiefs would have been had you *not* followed my advice?"

"But—" Primo says.

"Silence!" Zia Pia commands, and puts herself in a kind of wide-eyed trance. She then waves a candle above a bowl of water and searches its surface for images.

"I see a river . . . *our* river," Zia Pia says in a voice that sounds like it is coming from somewhere else. "It is night and a storm approaches, but I follow the water. . . . Up ahead I see the Bridge of Ancient Ages, and a fire . . . and—oh yes!—the Tree . . ."

She leans down to look more closely and

moves the flame right to the water. The fire lights up her nostrils.

"The Tree glows! And the Janara—they fly around it, like moths to the flame, circling, circling. There are hundreds of them! Thousands! And there are goblins! Spirits! Demons!"

"I see them, *too*!" Primo says, and Emilio jabs him in the ribs to shut up.

Taking a piece of paper and dipping a quill, Zia Pia closes her eyes and begins to draw.

"The Janara are strong this season—the strongest ever!" she says, blindly making marks. "It will take the *most* powerful spells I possess to slow them down."

When she is done, she pushes the paper toward Emilio and Primo. On it are strange writing and drawings. "Take this," she says, eyes still closed, "and go to the top of your barn. At the peak of the roof, place it under

three rocks
and say . . . *Ish
Ka-Bibble!*"

"Ish Ka-Bibble?"
Emilio says. "That's it?"

"*Ish Ka-Bibble!*"

Both boys reach to take
the drawing, but Zia Pia slaps her
hand down on top of it. "*Two* silver scudi," she
says, opening her eyes abruptly. "Or the dia-
gram stays with me."

"Give her the money!" Primo tells Emilio.
"That drawing is fan-*tas*-tic!"

Back at the farm, Rosa is *still* picking rocks,
and so bored out of her skull she is actually
happy to see Emilio, and even Primo. Her
cousin is waving a piece of paper above his
head, shouting, "Come look! Come look!"

"This will work for sure!" Rosa says after
hearing them explain the drawing, and she
insists on working the spell. "After all, it's *me*
who's in trouble."

The best climber in town, Rosa makes fast work of getting from her twin's shoulders onto the roof of the barn.

"Hurry!" Emilio calls up after her. "Before Father sees you!"

Primo and Emilio hear the quiet plinks of the stones getting set down and something being said. Then Rosa is back at the edge of the roof.

"It was *Nish-A-Diddly*, right?"

"No, it was *Ish Ka-Bibble*, you dope!" Emilio says.

"Just kidding!" Rosa says, and jumps down off the roof and rolls in the dirt.

That night, Father bolts and locks the window shutters and the front door so no one—namely Rosa—can get out of the house. (Even though the bolts were put there to keep bandits *out*, they do just as good a job of keeping children *in*.)

"I feel like I'm in prison," Rosa says.

The next morning, the loud unbolting of their window wakes up Emilio, who in turn wakes up his twin. As Father opens the shutters, they blink at the sudden sunlight and ask if anything happened during the night. Father grumbles an incomprehensible grumble, clearly unhappy, but not at Rosa.

The Twins walk over to the barn, go inside, and look up. All they see is sky, crisscrossed by beams. Every tile from the roof has been removed and flung into the fields. This is something Rosa would never have done and, moreover, *could* never have done, since she was locked inside all night.

"Do you think this is because of what we put on the roof?" Emilio whispers to Rosa.

"*Shhh!*" his twin says.

Paulo Pasquarelli has come

over to look at the scene. He shakes his head. "Worst darn case of Janara mischief I ever did see."

Rosa gives Father a smirk—not a good idea, Emilio thinks. Father pulls down the corner of his eye and walks away.

7

THE TREE OF THE JANARA

THE good news is that Rosa isn't grounded anymore. The *bad* news is that the mischiefs show no sign of stopping.

Rosa and Emilio spend all day with friends and neighbors fixing the barn roof, only to have an unpleasant surprise the next morning at breakfast when Dino opens the honey pot to find it filled not with honey but with **bees**.

The entire family knocks over dishes and chairs in a mad dash out of the house, a swarm of bees in pursuit. It ends with Father getting stung on the butt, and wanting to rip the hair out of his head. No one has any idea what to do. No one, that is, except Primo.

"You know what Zia Pia saw in the water, about the Bridge of Ancient Ages and the Janara and stuff?" Primo says. "What if we go to the Tree of the Janara for *real*?"

Primo thinks if they do go to the Tree, they can somehow convince the Janara to stop doing mischiefs at the farm. And even if they can't, he has something he believes will protect them from witches: the ring of a Manalonga.

At least, Primo *claims* it's the ring of a Manalonga. He found it in the belly of a fish, so everyone thinks it must be magic. But how can Primo know who it belonged to, let alone what it can do?

Nevertheless, Emilio finds himself sneaking out the bedroom window after Father and Momma have gone to sleep.

"Are you sure this is a good idea?" Emilio says to his twin, who is already charging ahead. "You just got *done* being grounded."

"Well, we have to try *something*," Rosa says, checking to make sure she's got her food and slingshot. "Besides, Primo's idea can't be worse than any of Zia Pia's. All she's done is make the Janara madder!"

Emilio isn't so sure about that. In fact, he is pretty sure that Primo's idea is a *lot* worse than any of Zia Pia's.

As he runs to keep up, all he can think of is the nursery rhyme Momma always told them:

On stormy nights the Janara ride
To the walnut tree that sits beside
The Bridge of Ancient Ages.

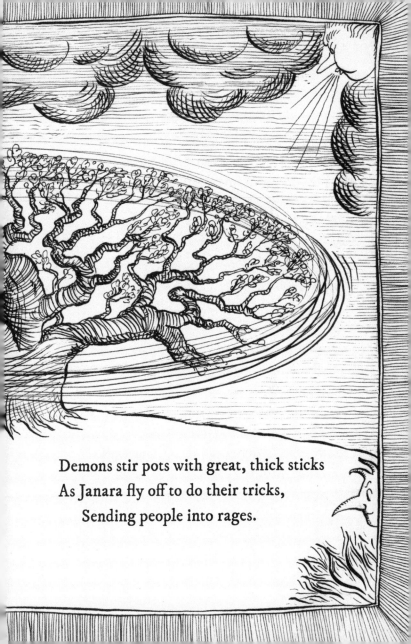

Demons stir pots with great, thick sticks
As Janara fly off to do their tricks,
    Sending people into rages.

Soon enough, the twins find themselves on the path upriver, following Primo's lead alongside Maria Beppina, and Sergio. Well, *sort* of Sergio.

"Don't you guys think it's time we should turn back?" Sergio says again. They have been walking along the river for nearly an hour. "We've been walking for *at least* two hours already, and we haven't seen anything!"

Maria Beppina would probably like to turn around and go home as much as Sergio, and so would Emilio. But since Emilio is the only one who's ever been to the Bridge of Ancient Ages,

WHICH TREE IS THE WITCH TREE?

Primo and Rosa won't let him.

Even so, Emilio has only been this far from home in the daytime, and only to hunt mushrooms. Speaking of which, there's a good one!

Emilio reaches down and plucks a big, juicy elephant's toe mushroom. It must be worth two quattrini, maybe three! He puts it in one of his pockets.

"Hey, donkey-brains, hurry up!" Rosa calls back. Doesn't her brother know something more important than fungus is going on here?

"How will we know which tree is the witch tree?" Maria Beppina asks.

"It will have walnuts, for one thing," Rosa says.

"And I heard it has a snakeskin hanging on it," Sergio adds.

"But won't the snakeskin be hard to see?" Maria Beppina asks. "What if we miss it?"

"Don't be stupid," Primo says. "We can't miss the Tree. It will have hundreds of *Janara* swarming around it!"

After passing an abandoned farm, the path disappears into a mix of brambles and woods. Pushing through, they come to a clearing where an old shepherd's hut made of stone stands empty.

"Let's stop for a snack," Rosa says. "I'm hungry!"

"You're *always* hungry!" Primo says.

"And let's make a fire," Sergio says. "I'm cold."

"Good idea!" Maria Beppina says.

"But we only *just* started walking!" Primo says, exasperated. "We have to keep going or we'll never get there!"

"We're **stopping**," Rosa says, and plunks her butt down on the ground. She takes out her roll of food, slices off a hunk of sausage, and sticks it inside a wedge of bread.

Emilio asks everyone to help with the fire, but Rosa says she's eating, like that's some sort of free pass. Her brother sighs and goes with Sergio and Maria Beppina to gather dead twigs and branches from an overgrown olive orchard on the other side of the hut.

Striking sparks from his flint, Emilio quickly lights a fire. The heat and smell of olive wood burning put everyone at ease.

"What do you think it's like?" Maria Beppina asks. "At the Tree."

"It's like a magnificent ball!" Rosa says. "The Janara wear red, white, and black gowns and ride in on flying kittens and bunnies. Then they dance around the Tree holding hands. And they are all beautiful! Like princesses."

"Princesses, **phooey!**" Primo says. "It's nothing like that. There are *men* Janara, too. And no kittens! They fly around on broomsticks and there are demons stirring cauldrons and stuff. It's *broomsticks* they use to fly, right, Emilio?"

"Actually, the brooms are just rudders, for steering," Emilio says. "Janara are made of wind, so they don't need help to fly."

"Well, *I* heard they fly in on kittens," Rosa says. "And bunnies!"

"Look, enough *talking* about what happens at the Tree," Primo says, getting up. "Let's go *find* it!" He kicks dirt on the fire.

They have been back walking for about five minutes when Primo stops and excitedly points up near the moon.

"I saw one! Right there! I *just* saw a Janara!"

Emilio wonders if Primo isn't making it up, but a few minutes later Rosa sees one, too. And she's *sure* it was a Janara, even if it was out of the corner of her eye and only for a second.

"And it was riding a kitten!"

When they arrive at the Bridge of Ancient Ages, it is not what either Primo or Rosa was hoping for.

"Where are the cauldrons?" Rosa says. "And Janara?"

"Are you sure we went far enough?" Primo says. "I don't think this is the right bridge!"

"It definitely is," Emilio says. "See, it has the head of the goat carved into it."

"So which tree is the witch tree?" Maria Beppina asks.

"That one!" Rosa says, pointing up a hill. "It's a walnut tree—just like it says in the rhyme! 'On *stormy nights the Janara ride to the **walnut** tree!*'"

"No way! It's *this* one," Primo says, walking to a tree right on the bank of the river. "It's so obvious!"

Rosa is annoyed. Everything always has to be *Primo's* discovery and *Primo's* way, even though he is always wrong about everything! "That's not even a walnut tree!"

"But it is *the tree that sits **beside** the Bridge of Ancient Ages*," Primo says. "Your tree is nowhere near the bridge!"

"Do either of them have a snakeskin on it?" Sergio says.

"*Forget* the snakeskin!" Primo says. "This is *way* more of a witches' tree than that one!"

"Like you'd know!" Rosa says.

First Sergio leaves—something about his ghost needing him—and then Maria Beppina follows.

"Fine! *Quitters!* Who needs you, anyway?" Primo calls after them. "I'm staying right here! There's going to be Janara *swarming* around this tree any minute."

"You mean *this* tree!"

Rosa says, climbing the walnut tree. "I'm gonna laugh when all the Janara come circling around me. Riding bunnies and kittens and dancing!"

"You two deserve each other!" Emilio says, shaking his head and walking off. "I'm joining the other two."

"You're just chicken, little cousin!" Primo calls after him, and starts clucking—*buk-buk-buk-BAAAWK!*—over and over. He then climbs into the tree he thinks is the right one. "I'm going to stay up all night if I have to, and when the Janara come, I'm going to tell them to do *more* mischiefs to your farm!"

Ignoring her cousin, Rosa takes out the rest of her bread and sausage and starts munching.

She can tell Primo is trying to ignore the food, but he must be starving! It was a long walk, after all, and he was the only kid who didn't bring anything to eat. Finally, he breaks down.

JUST A LITTLE BITE?

"Hey, Rosa, do you mind if I just have a piece of your bread?" Primo says, putting on his nicey-nicest voice. "Or even a little bite of sausage?"

"No way, donkey-brains! Why don't you just crack open some walnuts?" Rosa says. "Oh wait, you can't, because THAT'S NOT A WALNUT TREE!"

Meanwhile, Emilio is having no luck catching up with Maria Beppina and Sergio. How fast must they be walking?

When he gets to the clearing by the stone hut, Emilio finds the fire he made is still smoldering. He adds a few sticks, and the flames kick right back up. The warmth makes him sleepy, so he lies down in the shepherd's hut. *Ahh!* He yawns and closes his eyes. He can just walk back in the morning, he thinks, and falls asleep.

8

AMERIGO PEGLEG

IF the Twins really wanted to find Janara, they should have just stayed at home.

During the night, Janara attacked the cellar, unplugging casks of wine and turning them over. Father sets the kids to work sponging up the puddles of wine and squeezing the liquid into buckets.

"Bleck," Rosa says, wringing the dark purplish wine sludge out of her sponge. "Is Father *really* going to drink this?"

After a few more squeezes, Rosa curls up in a corner of the cellar to take a nap.

"Father is right," Dino says. "You *are* lazy."

"You try staying up all night in the crook

of a tree. My neck is killing me!" Rosa says, twisting it to one side. "Hey! Maybe the Janara *did* come to the Tree during the night, and they put this pain in my neck."

"*You* are a pain in the neck," Emilio says, but Rosa is somehow already asleep.

Emilio finishes the job with his little brother. "Why didn't you guys tell me you were going to the Tree?" Dino says. "You never let me do anything fun!"

"You're too *little*," Emilio says, pouring the last bucket of sopped-up wine into the barrel and plugging it. "Let's see what Father wants us to do next."

But for once he doesn't want them to do anything.

"Why bother?" Momma says, as much at wit's end as Father. "The Janara will just *un*do it!"

Leaving Dino to console their parents, Emilio heads off to town. As he approaches the gate, he hears the trumpet of Sergio's stepdad, the town crier.

> **Hear ye, hear ye!**
> It is the report of our government that the persistent cold weather threatens this year's crops. The lack of warmth is believed to be due to an uncommonly strong Dark Wind this spring. To compound the misfortune of our farmers, a rash of petty crime and vandalism has hit the countryside.

Oddly, no people have gathered to listen.
"Where is everybody?" Emilio asks.

The two of them find out exactly where everyone is as they walk together through the Theater to the crier's next assigned stop, the open area in front of Zia Pia's house. The line outside her door now winds all the way down the stairs and curls into the arena.

There is much grumbling from the waiting folks, and when an old man tries to cut the line, a fight breaks out. Sergio's stepdad gulps. He nervously raises the trumpet to his lips, and blows.

No one pays him any mind, so he sounds his horn louder and louder until his face turns red and he finally gets the attention of the crowd.

"Hear ye, hear ye!" the crier begins.
As soon as he talks about the
bad weather, however, a
farmer up the steps
cuts him off.

HEH!

"Why don't you tell us something we *don't* know, crier!"

Sergio's stepdad recovers·from the heckling and rattles off the part about the cold being the fault of the Dark Wind.

"The deuce it is!" a man from the back of the line yells. "**Janara** is what it is!"

The crier does his best to get through the rest of the text, but everything he says is shouted down. "Janara! Janara!" the crowd chants.

Insults begin getting hurled at the crier, and then something worse: donkey manure.

Sergio's stepdad ducks to avoid the clumps of donkey dung being aimed at his head. The scene turns into a brouhaha, and the poor man runs for his life.

Amidst the commotion, Emilio hears a familiar voice.

"I hope you didn't come to waste any more of your money, boy."

Amerigo Pegleg points his cane up to Zia Pia's apartment. "This half-wit fraud doesn't know the first thing about Janara!"

"Is it true you went to America?" Emilio asks.

Amerigo looks surprised by the change of subject, or maybe by someone being interested in him.

"Of course I went to America!" Amerigo says, his bluster returning. "With a name like Amerigo, how could I not? I wouldn't let an ocean stop me!"

"And did you really fight in the war there?" Emilio says.

"The Revolution, you mean!" Amerigo says, banging his chest with a fist. "I served under General George Washington himself. He was like a father to me!"

"And how did your—" Emilio starts to say. "That is, well . . ."

"How did my leg get blown off, you mean? A cannonball!" the old soldier says, tapping his wooden limb, which used to be the leg of a fancy table.

When Emilio next asks if he was a pirate like some kids say, Amerigo laughs—a happy, roaring laugh. "You sure have a lot of questions, boy!" he says. "I like you."

A look of kind concern comes to Amerigo's face as he rubs his stubbly chin. "Are the Janara still bothering your farm?" he asks.

"Worse than ever," Emilio says.

Amerigo nods his head. "Come," he says.

Leaning heavily on his cane, the old soldier wobbles to stand and starts to walk. Emilio follows him out through the city gate, throwing the horns to the ground and spitting.

When they get to the bridge, Amerigo goes right up its ramp. *Thump thump thump,* his peg leg sounds as it strikes the stones. At the peak of the bridge, he sits on the edge, at the very spot where Manalonga are *known* to have snatched children.

Is he crazy? He wants to have a chat *there*?

"Don't worry!" Amerigo calls to Emilio. "It's safe."

Walking up the ramp, Emilio desperately wants to stick his fingers in his ears and sing *LA-la-la-la-La*. The roar of the water below slowly forms into a voice. Rosa's voice.

Hey, Emilio! Come look! I found the most amazing thing down here. It's a golden mushroom! Come on, donkey-brains. **Look!**

Emilio's hair stands on end and he freezes where he stands, but Amerigo leans over the edge and bellows,

"Oh, pipe down, you infernal hell-hag! Go bother someone who's a-scared of your tricks!"

From below the bridge come a series of screeching, in-human shrieks, which slowly die away.

"How did you *do* that?" Emilio says.

Amerigo waves away the question with his hand. "You must swear never to tell *anyone* what I am about to tell you, least of all your sister or your friends." He pokes Emilio hard in the chest. "*Especially* your friends."

"I swear," Emilio says, holding one hand to his heart and the other in the air.

"If I told you I was a Janara, my life would no longer be worth living," Amerigo says. "Only here—in the presence of the Manalonga—do I dare tell you anything at all."

Amerigo Pegleg is a Janara? Is that what he

is trying to tell me? Emilio thinks. *Could it be?*

"Why do we have to talk in the presence of a Manalonga?" Emilio says.

"So none of *them* will hear," Amerigo says, looking up toward the sky. "Even Janara are afraid of Manalonga!"

"But why aren't *you* afraid?"

Amerigo smiles. "There are different types of Janara, my boy, just as there are different types of men." He leans in closer and talks in a whisper. "You may *think* you know about Janara, but you don't. We—I mean, *they*—are like knights of the world beyond. The Revolution in America was the *second* war I fought. The first was far more dangerous."

"Who did you fight?" Emilio says. "In the first war. Other Janara?"

"I can tell you no more, boy. I have already told you too much!" Amerigo says, shaking his head. "Here is what I can say: no one can fight the Janara and win. Not at their own game—not at night—and not unless you are called to be a Janara yourself. Garlic and silly rhymes will only make them angry."

Amerigo grabs Emilio by the arm, his long fingernails sharp against the boy's skin. "Janara are like bees. They can fly, make sweet mischiefs like honey, and bring forth the very spring itself. But when mad"—Amerigo pinches Emilio hard enough to make him wince—"we *sting*!"

Emilio pulls back his arm, the top of which hurts from the pinch. "So how do I make the Janara happy?" Emilio asks, rubbing his shoulder.

Amerigo wets his lips. He whispers, "Oregano."

"What?" Emilio says. "What do you mean, *oregano?*"

"Take oregano to the places where the Janara have come. Brush it everywhere. The smell is like catnip for them—it makes them happy. They will move on to some other place to do their mischiefs."

"And that's it?"

Amerigo nods. "That's it."

Emilio goes to ask another question, but the old peg-legged soldier cuts him off. "I've already told you too much!" he repeats, but this time nervously. "Remember—say nothing to your friends! One of them lives with a Jan—"

Amerigo catches himself before he says anything more and disappears *thump thump thump* back down the bridge.

9

A WHIFF OF OREGANO

AS Emilio rubs and brushes dried sprigs of oregano on the posts of the barn, he keeps playing over in his mind what he just heard.

Amerigo Pegleg is a Janara? It seems impossible. Of course, *someone* has to be a Janara, so why not him?

On the other hand, maybe he is just a crazy old man. Or is Emilio the crazy one for doing what he told him to? Could oregano possibly keep the Janara away? He's got nothing to lose, though, so he keeps rubbing away. It *does* smell good.

The barn done, Emilio goes and opens the cellar door. Down inside, he finds Rosa, still

curled up in the corner. He pushes her awake with his foot.

"Have you been sleeping here *all* day?"

"Is it still daytime?" Rosa says, yawning. "It's so dark down here." She stretches. "Hey, what are you doing?"

"I'm rubbing oregano on the wine barrels."

"What?" she says. *"Why?"*

"Because someone told me it would cure our Janara problem."

"Who told you?" Rosa asks.

"I can't tell."

"It was Zia Pia, wasn't it?"

"I can't *tell*, I said," Emilio says. "But no."

"Then it was Primo. It sounds just like another one of his dopey ideas!"

Emilio refuses to say anything more. Annoyed at a secret being kept from her, Rosa gets up from the floor and dusts herself off.

"Rubbing oregano everywhere sure as heck won't do anything," she says. "So I guess I'm going to have to take care of things."

She picks up a stick and begins drawing a picture in the dirt floor.

"Is that a horse?" Emilio says.

"No, donkey-brains! It's a dog."

"Why are you drawing a picture of a dog?"

"Because everyone knows that Janara are afraid of dogs."

"No they aren't!"

"Not *real* dogs," Rosa says. "Spirit dogs! Because of the way Janara ride around on kittens and bunnies."

"So what's drawing a picture of a dog going to do?"

"A lot more than rubbing oregano everywhere!" Rosa says. "You just have to listen to your big sister for once."

"You are *not* my big sister. We're twins.

Just because you pushed yourself out six minutes before me doesn't make you any older."

"Yes it does!" she says. "Besides, I didn't say
I was older, I said I was bigger." Which is true,
but it was still obnoxious.

Rosa stands back to admire her work, but
something isn't right. Oh yeah, a spell!

Her nose twists into a knot for a minute. It
always does that when she is thinking hard.

"Oh Spirit of Dog,
Please bark in the night,
And growl at the moon,
To send Janara in flight!"

Rosa nods. "There, that should do it."

Emilio gives up on his twin and goes upstairs to oregano their room, while Rosa goes
to the barn to draw more dog pictures.

The next morning, the Twins don't wake
up to their father screaming, or angry. When
they find him, he's smiling. *Actually* smiling.
What can it mean?

Baffled, they go into the barn. The smell of oregano lingers in the air. Rather than being torn apart, the barn has been cleaned. Even the straw looks arranged.

"Hey, Emilio, come look at this!" Rosa says.

In the stalls, Ugo the ox and Poca the mule have been groomed, with their manes and tails braided and tied off in pretty ribbons.

"Look!" Dino says, entering with a crate. "Eggs! And the fields are *full* of greens!"

Amerigo Pegleg isn't crazy—he really *did* know how to fix the mischiefs! Emilio can hardly believe it.

"See," Rosa says. "I knew it would work."

"No, you didn't," Emilio says. "You said the oregano was ridiculous."

"I'm not talking about the oregano, donkey-brains!" she says. "I'm talking about my dog pictures!"

"You can't be serious!" Emilio says.

"What? You think the oregano your mystery friend told you about is what fixed it? Yeah, right!" Rosa takes Ugo out of his stall and starts hooking him up to the cart while Dino loads it up with crates of eggs and fennel greens. "I can't wait to go tell Primo how I chased off the Janara!"

"Can I come?" Dino asks.

"Sure!" Rosa says.

Father is so happy he actually gives them the day off. Emilio can hardly believe it! With his unexpected free time, he decides to go

mushroom hunting. It is always when he does his best thinking.

If Amerigo Pegleg was right about the oregano, what else does he know? Emilio can't get the last thing the old soldier said out of his head:

Say nothing to your friends! One of them lives with a Jan—

Did he mean *Janara*? What else could he mean? But if he did, who is it? Could Sergio be right about his mom? Or how about Nonna Jovanna, Primo's grandma? Or Primo's mom, Aunt Zufia? Nah, it *can't* be her—she's too normal!

Emilio thinks about asking Primo's sister

Isidora—she seems to know things about Janara—but then he remembers he is sworn to secrecy. Oh well, he'll just have to figure it out for himself. Emilio does love mysteries.

Life goes on, but our book is done!

WELL, well, well—I never saw that coming. Oregano! Who'd have thought? (Or was it Rosa's dog drawings that changed the Janara's mood?)

Of course, there are so many other questions!

Is Amerigo Pegleg really a Janara?

Is one of our friends actually living with a Janara? (See, I told you they could be someone you know.)

What did happen to Sergio and Maria Beppina on their walk home from the Bridge of Ancient Ages?

Why was there a ring inside of a fish?

Emilio would love to learn the answers to these questions, but YOU can! There are more books for you to read, and beyond merely satisfying your curiosity, you can actually go inside the heads of Primo, Maria Beppina, and Sergio.

Haven't you ever wanted to do that? To know what your friends are really thinking? Now is your chance!

Sigismondo

RAFAELLA

BRUNO

S.   R.   B.

WITCHONARY

—⊹—

IN Benevento, any kind of supernatural being is called a witch. And boy, are there a *lot* of them.

The Clopper: An old witch believed to be the last of her particular kind. She haunts the open square of the Theater, chasing children who dare cross it. Every kid in Benevento knows the *clop clop clop* of her one wooden clog!

Demons: Wily magical creatures who live among humans disguised as animals. In Benevento, 1 in 7 cats are demons, unless they are black, in which case it's 2 out of 3. Dogs, on the other hand, are never demons. Goats almost always are.

Ghosts: Spirits of those who died before their time. They must be taken care of by the descendants in whose homes they dwell. (Also called Ancestor Spirits.)

Goblins: Animal-like creatures whom Janara often keep as pets.

Janara: (Juh-NAHR-uh) Certain men and women can transform themselves into this type of witch by rubbing a magic oil into their armpits and saying a spell, after which they fly off to their famous tree to start a night of mischiefs. Janara belong to a secret society and don't dare reveal their secret identities to anyone!

Manalonga: (Man-uh-LONG-uh) The most feared of all witches. They lurk under bridges or inside wells and try to snatch children for unknown (but surely sinister) purposes.

Mares: A type of goblin who sits on children's chests at night, causing bad dreams.

Spirits: Witches who have no earthly bodies and live in one particular place, be it a house, chimney, stream, or arch. Types of spirits include ghosts, house fairies, and water sprites.

Life was very different in
Benevento in the 1820s.

HERE'S HOW THEY LIVED.

- ❖ Kids didn't go to school, they worked.
  They still learned; it was just how to be a
  craftsman, like a baker or a candlemaker.

- ❖ Could kids read? No way! Not many of
  them, anyway. Their parents couldn't read
  either. Reading was considered weird.

- ❖ They couldn't count very high, or do math
  in their heads. (But they did know how to
  start a fire with nothing but a few twigs
  and a flint.)

- ❖ Credit cards and paper money didn't exist.
  To pay for something, you had to use coins,
  which were mostly made of copper (for
  little things) and silver (for big things).
  Only really rich folks had gold coins.

- Folks learned what was going on in the world from town criers. For entertainment, kids listened to storytellers or musicians who sang stories, or went to puppet shows.

- Windows didn't have glass in them—they were just holes in the side of buildings. Glass was too expensive!

- Straws weren't invented yet, at least not the plastic kind. But there was real straw, which is made from dried, hollow stalks of grass. It works just as well for sucking up drinks! (Well, almost.)

- Most people never lived anywhere but the home they were born in. Some never left the town they were born in. Not even once.

If you want to learn MORE, please visit www.witchesofbenevento.com.

HISTORICAL NOTE

THE WITCHES OF BENEVENTO is set in 1820s Benevento.

Benevento was an important crossroads in Roman times and was the capital of the Lombards in Southern Italy during the early Middle Ages.

Even before the Romans conquered it, the town was famous as a center of witches. (Its original name, Maleventum—"bad event"—was switched by the Romans to Beneventum—"good event"—in hope of changing things. It didn't work.) For hundreds of years, Benevento was believed to be the place where all the witches of the world gathered, attending their peculiar festivals at a walnut tree near the Sabato River.

The people of Benevento, however, never believed there was anything wrong with witches, and maybe that's why they had—or thought they had—so many of them.

JOHN BEMELMANS MARCIANO

I grew up on a farm taking care of animals. We had one spectacularly nice chicken, the Missus, who lived in a stall with an ancient horse named Gilligan, and one rooster, Leon, who pecked our heads on our way home from school. Leon, I have no doubt, was a demon. Presently I take care of two cats, one dog, and a daughter.

SOPHIE BLACKALL

I've illustrated many books for children, including the Ivy and Bean series. I drew the pictures in this book using ink made from black olives and goat spit. I grew up in Australia, but now my boyfriend and I live in Brooklyn with a cat who never moves and a bunch of children who come and go like the wind.

Read all the books in the
WITCHES of BENEVENTO
series!

THE ALL-POWERFUL RING:
A Primo Story

Primo hopes to prove he is the bravest of the children by confronting the Manalonga, who lurk under bridges and in wells. When he finds a ring inside a fish, he believes it is magic and will protect him from harm. Is he right?

Coming Soon!
BEWARE THE CLOPPER!
A Maria Beppina Story

Maria Beppina, the shy little tagalong, is always afraid that the Clopper, the old witch who chases the children, will catch her. And then one day she decides to stop—just stop—and see what the Clopper will do.

Coming Soon!
RESPECT YOUR GHOSTS:
A Sergio Story

Sergio is in charge of the ancestor spirit who lives upstairs. Unfortunately, the many, many demands of the ghost make it impossible for Sergio to keep him happy.